# BÊTE NOIRE

## FEAR IS JUST A POINT OF VIEW

Editors:

A. W. Gifford

Jennifer L. Gifford

P.O. Box 1545
Highland, MI 48357

www.betenoiremagazine.com

Bête Noire is published by Dark Opus Press a division of Charm Noir Omnimedia P.O Box 1545, Highland, MI 48357

ISBN: 978-0692231500

# In This Issue

# BLACK

## Sorcha Dubh

Black. Deep, complete blackness.

It surrounded him, enveloped him, smothered him. There was nothing but darkness; darkness and pain. The pain came upon him suddenly, illuminated by the neon glow of his awakening consciousness. It lanced through his back, bright, burning slashes of agony in his otherwise dark and featureless world. In a strange way he was glad of it, this agony; it was something to hold on to, something to feel.

He was lying on a hard and unyielding surface. Confusion blinded him, clouding his memories. Did he remember a cave? He thought he could recall himself climbing, clambering through the darkness. He grappled with the mental image of a struggle, of a journey from darkness towards light. But there was no light here. He laid still, prone on the rocky floor, his tender skin feeling every knife-like chip and stone beneath him. Something else lay across him, an oppressive weight, pinning his legs and compressing his chest. It hurt to breathe. How did he get here?

He tried to move, to shift the weight from his body and relieve the pressure on his lungs. He dug his shoulder blades into the ground, the gravel clawing his skin, and tried to push upwards. A new, deeper pain sliced through him, shooting along his ribs. He moaned soundlessly, the few reserves of strength draining from his muscles. His breath came in short, frantic gasps. How badly was he hurt?

The dryness of his throat burned him, and his breath scraped across it more viciously than the gravel on which he lay. He tried to cry out but his voice crumbled to a cracked, wordless croaking. Swallowing, he tried to moisten his mouth and tongue with chalky, stone-flavoured saliva. The dust coated his throat and he gave a hollow cough. He listened, ears straining, for far longer than he should have, but he could hear no echo. The sound radiated forlornly into the black, but the darkness around him responded only with silence.

Suppressing panic he cleared his throat again and tried to cry out, louder than before. This time his voice was stronger, fuller. He waited, but again only a deep and empty silence answered him. For a moment longer he fought the rising panic...then he surrendered to it. Pinned as he was he thrashed about, oblivious to the pain in his body. Even that frenzied energy could not so much as shift the rocks that trapped him. His muscles screamed as they were wrenched from side to side, and the rocks beneath him tore strips from his skin. His skull thumped against the rock floor until bright lights flashed before his eyes. His screams pierced the stillness, hot knives scraping along his barren throat. Finally, exhausted, he lay still and gasped for breath. His lungs were furnaces in his chest. His ribs ached as if they had been beaten and searing pain lanced his back. He let his head fall back to the rock and stared into the blackness.

Black. Silence. He closed his eyes. He opened them. There was no perceptible difference. He must have fallen asleep or perhaps passed out. It was hard to tell which. But now he was awake; the dull throbs of pain from his ribs and back confirmed that. Unless he was dreaming... for a moment he grappled with the idea that this might all be a dream, and he was asleep somewhere, safe and warm. He wanted desperately for it to be true. Could he wake himself up? He struggled to remember times in the past when he had awoken from dreams. He tried twitching, jerking, as much as he could in the confines of his prison. He tried blinking, he tried not blinking, staring at the darkness until his eyes burned. His desperation spurred him on. Finally, defeated, he relented. A fatalistic calm swept through him. Was he dreaming? If so, he could not wake.

He consoled himself that at least the pain seemed to be easing. It was still there, but it was no longer pressing. He found that he could choose whether to focus on it or ignore it. Did that mean it was getting better or worse? He tried to shift position, to ease his stiffening joints, but it was impossible. He called out just to break the silence, and imagined his voice to be a glowing, brilliant dove, venturing out bravely through the oppressive darkness. But this dove did not return bearing symbols of promise. He felt a sliver of hope shrink within him.

Thirst tormented him. His throat had grown even drier than before, parched and leathery, it strangled his breath. Even his chalk-dust saliva had dissipated, leaving him with a swollen, pebble-stuffed tongue. How long had he been there? He realised that he could not say. In this world of darkness it was almost impossible to tell one moment from the next, just as it was impossible to tell sleep from wakefulness, dreaming from reality. Could his thirst be some measure of time, some indication of the duration of his imprisonment? Or perhaps even that, that suffocating barren thirst, was a frantic imagining, a product of his desperation.

He closed his eyes. He opened them. There was no perceptible difference. How long had he been there now? Had he slept? Again, it was impossible to say. He did not know if he had slept for an hour or ten, or if a momentary lapse in concentration had stretched to some imagined infinity. In this perfect stillness the only thing he had to mark the passing of time was his own breath. In and out, in and out. It was a mantra, a meditation, a prayer. His mind wandered. In a silent nothingness the smallest activity becomes central, essential. If he held his breath would time stand still?

He could no longer feel the rocks, or the pain. There was no sound, no light, no colour. He felt as if he was floating in a void of perfect stillness. Somehow the darkness was no longer threatening. It simply was, and it was all there was.

But his complacency was short-lived. Devoid as he was of all sensation, a sudden panic gripped him. Where was he? Why couldn't he feel anything? He felt the darkness close tightly around him, an eternal, colourless silence rushing to engulf him. He was submerged in darkness, smothering. He screamed reflexively, the sudden sound jerking him from his panic. It reverberated around him, a cocoon of sound expanding into the surrounding emptiness. It anchored him, rooted him, a glowing tendril of reality gripping him and pulling him from the void. He began to laugh with relief and again the sound rippled around him, populating the vacuum, sweeping away the black. He began to talk, to chatter, to sing; a constant stream of sound, of life, of existence. He clung to the sound, knowing that if it were to cease the nothingness would claim him once more.

Time passed. He was telling himself a story, reliving an old memory, but the details seemed jumbled and shifted constantly. He could see the images forming and dissipating in his mind, hear his thoughts rattling incoherently through his brain. He stopped. Silence. He was not speaking, had not been speaking for some time now. The voice in his mind rippled on. A wave of relief surged through him. He was still here, he still existed; the darkness had not claimed him. He almost felt ecstatic, for now he knew that there was nothing to fear. He lay there, silently drifting, listening to the thoughts in his mind, to the sound of himself living, being.

Ideas and memories raced across his consciousness, thoughts and emotions dancing across the darkness. Vivid and vibrant, the blackness only served to make them shine more brightly. A thought rippled across his perception, almost too quick for him to process. What if... Intrigued, he reached for it, testing it, feeling it shifting like a fish beneath his grasping consciousness. He focused on the elusive thought, and regretted his decision almost instantly. But there it was, stronger now and rising to the surface, casting all other thoughts out into the darkness. What if...what if I am already dead?

His breath caught. All was silence and emptiness. He willed himself to breathe, in and out, out and in. How did he know he was still alive? He tried to move, but he could feel nothing. He tried to speak, but there was no sound. There was nothing, absolutely nothing, but a single solitary voice in his mind. He was his thoughts and nothing more. Had he died without noticing? A crushing despair engulfed him. Perhaps he had died and passed into nothingness. Only his consciousness remained. But for how long? An eternity of isolation, watching his thoughts dancing and shifting and rambling through the darkness? Or the alternative, a gradual dispersal, a voice fading to a whisper, the silence from without reaching within to claim him.

And then, unbidden, a second idea followed the first, rising from the blackest recesses of his mind. The thought hit him with a resounding, sickening finality. How did he know that he had ever really existed at all? He would have gasped, but he had no awareness of his breath anymore. When he thought he had spoken, had he been dreaming, imagining it? Had he ever been anything more than a voice in the darkness? How could he know? It seemed that his life had never been anything other than here, now, emptiness and silence and darkness. Could he test the reality of a memory, of a dream? Surely, surely there was some way to know.... Panic rose to the surface now, filling the pool of his thoughts. Was this all he was? All he ever would be? A mind, a stream of thoughts, here alone in the darkness... forever?

What would happen if he stopped thinking? Could he? No. No, there must be something, someone, anyone else. He was trapped beneath some rocks and it was very dark, that was the reality he must cling to. But even that may have been an invention of his mind. There was nothing and no one, and no way to know. And this was his reality, now and forever. Terror claimed him and he screamed and screamed and screamed. He did not know if he could hear himself, or if he simply heard his mind screaming. He did not know anything. There was terror and panic, and then there was no thought.

Silence. No thinking. No mind.

Light.

*Sorcha Dubh is an Irish writer, who works primarily in the fantasy and literary fiction genres. She is currently working on her first novel, provisionally titled* The Betrayed, *which is set to be the first volume in a high fantasy trilogy exploring the far-reaching and devastating effects of acts of betrayal within families. She is also putting the final touches to* The Question, *a self-contained short story collection.*

# The Mad Hatter at Large

## Marge Simon

Today I am your friend, Alice.
Watch for a white door with a red X.
When and if you find it,
beware the sign that says OPEN ME,
count to three hundred seven
& don't turn the handle to the right.

I've taught the joys
of tearing wings off insects
to Tweedles Dum & Dee,
particularly those of butterflies
& wayward fairies.

I've drowned the Dormouse
in the Pool of Tears, served him
to the Queen of Hearts in a stew.
She seemed to enjoy his tiny skull
floating in a sea of vomit.

I've  reset the clocks
that determine lifetimes,
assuring that kindly people
will live fairly long and prosper,
though covered with unsightly warts

& self-inflicted wounds.

Dear me, did I forget to warn you
not to eat these pretty mushrooms?
Their potent juices take effect
within forty-eight hours.
Alas, you'll soon be blind.

Plotting your death in a most
disgustingly gruesome manner,
the white rabbit relaxes in his deck chair,
sipping Margaritas on the beach
of a posh Oahu hotel.

Marge Simon's *works appear in publications such as* Strange Horizons,
Niteblade, DailySF Magazine, Pedestal Magazine, Dreams & Night-
mares. *She edits a column for the HWA Newsletter and serves as Chair of
the Board of Trustees. She has won the Strange Horizons Readers Choice
Award, the Bram Stoker Award™(2008, 2012, 2013), the Rhysling Award
and the Dwarf Stars Award. Collections:* Like Birds in the Rain, Unearthly
Delights, The Mad Hattery, Vampires, Zombies & Wanton Souls, *and*
Dangerous Dreams. Member HWA, SFWA, SFPA. *www.margesimon.com*

ALICE IN WONDERLAND *by Luke Spooner*

Luke Spooner *a.k.a. 'Carrion House' currently lives and works in the South of England. Having recently graduated from the University of Portsmouth with a first class degree he is now a full time illustrator for just about any project that peaks his interest. Despite regular forays into children's books and fairy tales his true love lies in anything macabre, melancholy or dark in nature and essence. He believes that the job of putting someone else's words into a visual form, to accompany and support their text, is a massive responsibility as well as being something he truly treasures.*

*www.carrionhouse.com*
*www.facebook.com/carrionhouse*

# DETERGENT

## Siobhan Gallagher

The red light went off. Zef hurried from room to room and tied down any loose items.

"Honey?" he called out.

"I've got the living room," said his wife. "Grandma's secured in her wheelchair."

Just as he was coming down the hallway, gravity lost its hold. He grabbed the railing before he bumped into the ceiling. Damn gravity unit was on the fritz again. When were they ever going to fix it — and his garbage disposal, too?

From the laundry room, dirty unmentionables floated out. Great, just great. He swung himself over, grabbed a fistful of items, including his man-thong — couldn't have the kids asking questions about *that*. And while he was here, he might as well do the laundry. So he shoved the clothes into the washer and reached for the detergent —

Empty.

Mother of God, could nothing go right today?

He poked his head out the laundry room. "Honey, we're out of detergent."

"Already?" she called back.

"Well grandpa wasn't a big guy — he didn't exactly leave us much." He then spotted grandma from across the hallway. She was snoring away; her robotic hearing aid rested on her shoulder, a curled up metallic roach.

Since she wasn't doing anything useful, might as well turn her in. In all honesty, they should've done it years ago, to help keep down the population and conserve resources, but his wife *insisted* on keeping the old wind-bag. He put on a pair of sticky boots and shuffled over to grandma, pocketed her hearing aid — she wouldn't be needing it where she was going. He started undoing the straps that held her down.

Joseph stuck his head into the living room. "Hey dad, when's the grav coming back?"

"Shh." He waved him off. "I don't know, but be quie—"

"What are you doing?" His wife clung to the entryway. Every few seconds, she swiped a hovering lock of hair away from her face.

"Uh..." He looked from her to his son. "Joseph, go find your brother. Now's a perfect time to play some zero-ball."

Joseph's eyes lit up, seeing an opportunity. "Can we have some credits for the arcade?"

"Sure, sure. There's a card in my desk."

Joseph disappeared, leaving him with his wife and her disapproving look.

"We need detergent so—"

"How could you?" She frowned. "You should at least wait until she dies."

He sighed. "But that's taking too long. We need soap *now*."

"Absolutely not!"

"I think we've kept her long enough, past her usefulness anyway. What does she do now? Except cost us credits. I mean, how many hips do we have to replace on her?"

"She's not a refrigerator."

"I agree. Our fridge has never given us trouble."

"That's not what I mean." Her forehead wrinkled, and she was looking a little too much like her mother. "It's inhumane to do it so soon."

He threw up his hands. "Inhumane is not having any clean underwear."

Grandma stirred and he froze. The old wind-bag smacked her dry lips and muttered something, then settled back into her snores. What exactly did his wife see in her? Sentimental value, maybe?

"Look," he said, "I hear there's a very nice room on the station, they'll give her some juice, play her favorite music and she won't notice a thing."

"I just can't imagine getting rid of grandma like that."

"I can."

"Oh Zef." She gave a slight shake of her head. "You wouldn't want someone doing that to *you*."

He stood straight, proud. "Honey, when it's my time to become soap, it's my time. I'm not going to deny my family their right to clean clothes. Besides," he said, and reached out to his wife, "would you really miss her? All her nagging and telling you, you shouldn't wear low-cut dresses. As soap she'll finally be of some use."

She still kept to the wall, wearing that frown. Time for some other tactics.

"Okay, if you won't let me turn her in, then we're just going to have to buy that low-grade brand."

Her eyes widened. "Oh God no."

"Oh yes. Paying out the ass for something we could get for free. And no telling *who* it's made from."

Her brows furrowed in concentration. Ah, he had her now, just needed to drive it home. He waved her over. "Come smell her."

"What?"

"It's fine, just come."

His wife glided over and he took her arm to steady her. She leaned over and took a whiff of grandma's curly greys. "Reminds me of the smoky springs on Cernol-5."

He put his face close to hers. "Your clothes could smell like that."

She smiled a little, but her eyes held unease. "I don't know..."

"Think of it this way: You won't be losing a grandmother, you'll be gaining some laundry soap."

"You might be right... But what will the boys say?"

"Between games and checking out girls, they won't even notice."

She nodded. "If there's any left over, maybe we can use her for some bubble soap."

"Sure!"

As though it were sign from the heavens, the light blinked from red to green. He grabbed his wife by the waist and gravity returned. Somehow, things always had a way of working out — and good thing: he was on his last pair of clean underwear.

"All right, help me with these straps," he said. "And if she wakes up, tell her we're going for a walk."

Siobhan Gallagher *is a wannabe zombie slayer, currently residing in south Texas. Her fiction has appeared in several publications, including* AE - The Canadian Science Fiction Review, COSMOS Online, Abyss & Apex, *and* Unidentified Funny Objects *anthology.*

# Florence Grey

These bones were useful once.
a chalk dust display of a lie now
laid to rest—
at least to me.
Even now,
as the moon shines through your
skulls eye I still feel your gaze upon me.
Longing to speak the words on lips
I'll never kiss again, as I drop down
to kiss your forehead—bleached white by the light
of the sun—and drop in the ring you gave me
into the dirt and dusty unknown,
where the wind and the ages
will blow your lies to dust.

*Florence Grey has been writing poetry for nearly twenty years. She loves the swing and big band era and prefers writing her poetry with pen and paper to that of a computer.*

**KiDS WiTH GuNS** *by Eleanor Leonne Bennett*

Eleanor Leonne Bennett *is a sixteen year old internationally award winning photographer and artist who has won first places with* National Geographic, The World Photography Organization, Nature's Best Photography, Papworth Trust, Mencap, The Woodland Trust *and* Postal Heritage. *Her photography has been published in the Telegraph ,* The Guardian, BBC News Website *and on the cover of books and magazines in the United states and Canada. Her art is also globally exhibited.*

# JEREMY

## Addison Clift

New Year's morning and my head was pounding. I sat out by the far end of the pool and sipped a tall cup of coffee. The day was so heavy and grey you could barely see Century City in the mist, and even this was too much for my aching eyeballs. But every time I closed my eyes that face appeared to me. His face.

The party went pretty well considering that Rachel and I are barely speaking outside of Dr. Kaufmann's. The only important cancellation was a last minute from Lily and Jane. Lou Paretsky continued his annual tradition of trying to stump me with film trivia. "Alan," he said, "I've got a good one for you. Bob Hoskins once said to Michael Caine, 'There have been three great British crime films. I was in one, you were in one, and we both were in the other.' What were the films?"

I didn't even need to think about it. "Hoskins was in *The Long Good Friday*, Caine was in *Get Carter*, and they were both in *Mona Lisa*. You're going to have to do a lot better than that if you want to stump me."

He grimaced. Shaken but undeterred, he tried again. "Um...why couldn't they use a prop door on *The Shining*?"

"Nicholson was a volunteer firefighter. He blew through their breakaway with one whack. Also, 'Here's Johnny' was ad-libbed and Kubrick didn't know what the hell it meant. They didn't get The Tonight Show in England."

Lou conceded defeat and toasted his cinematic superior, but no sooner had he slumped away than Keith Gordon pulled me aside to ask about funding for *The Living and the Dead*. I stalled him, then made my escape. I found that the best way to avoid people I didn't have answers for was to get my camera and hide behind it. I took more than two hundred pictures. Rachel was in nine of them. So was Jeremy Rice.

I'm sure it was him. There is no doubt in my mind. I spent hours studying the photo from his obituary.

From the notes of Dr. Yedida Kaufmann, PhD:

*Per Rachel, affair began after Alan refused to attend open mic reading. She met Jeremy Rice there, was moved by his poetry. When Alan learned of affair he was outraged, insisted she break it off. She says she did right away, Alan says it went on two more weeks. After she ended it, Rice made several attempts to contact her but was rebuffed. Rice bought gun at pawn shop and committed suicide. Was found by roommate. Alan afraid that if his name gets tied to this, would be all over press. Rachel said don't flatter yourself, press hasn't cared about you in ten years. Alan then accused Rachel of only setting up these appointments because it will look good in court.*

*End of session. No progress made.*

Saturday was Moishe Lieberman's granddaughter's bat mitzvah. I don't even know the little brat's name. I was a witness to her transition to womanhood because most of the private equity firms we deal with had politely declined, while Lieberman Media Group was still, technically, a maybe.

Moishe avoided me before the ceremony. I finally cornered him in the parking lot afterward as the kids piled into limousines for the dance party.

"You have no North American pre-sales," he said in his wheezy, imperious voice. "And you've been reduced to running around Europe acting as your own sales agent." Moishe had a knack for making me feel like I was still learning the ropes in this business; nonetheless I was surprised he knew where I'd been. He continued. "And when we talked in the fall, my understanding was that this would be a Holocaust picture."

I braced myself before going into my spiel, since his father was a survivor. Still, I knew Moishe appreciated frankness. "There's no audience for Holocaust movies anymore," I told him. "They've lost the Academy's interest, too. That's just the blunt truth. But this puts a twist on it. I mean, how could so many nations turn all those refugees away? This is the Shoah, the Diaspora, and the partition all in one. It's high concept drama, and it's the kind of thing that gets noticed. This will be an important film."

Moishe just shook his head, clucking softly. "You've had three directors come and go, you managed to lose both the Gyllenhaals, and your pre-sales are nonexistent. Whenever I hear anyone talk about *The Living and the Dead* it's always the same thing: stay away, it'll never get out of development hell."

I don't know what it was that sent me into a funk—Moishe's open use of the H-word, or the fact that I knew it was true. I'd been kidding myself for too long, and not just about this project. They might as well have said stay away from Alan Levy. They probably are, when they know I'm not around.

On the way home from the bat mitzvah I passed the Starbucks on Santa Monica where he used to work. On some brooding impulse I went in.

I didn't see any photos or sympathy cards, so I asked the girl at the counter if she'd known someone named Jeremy Rice. She paled. I said I was a former professor of his (though I wasn't even sure if he'd gone to college) and I added that "he wrote beautiful poetry."

This opened her up. She said everyone was in shock. I asked her what happened. She said Jeremy was in love, really in love, with this married woman. "I told him to be careful, but he insisted it was real. He said she loved him too. He would sit in here all day and fill notebook after notebook with poetry, just for her. I know—what a hopeless romantic, right?"

"A married woman."

"Yeah. Supposedly the husband was a real prick."

"Oh."

"Do you want to hear something he wrote?" I nodded. She quoted from memory. "Every star you see is already gone/And the dark sky is filled with secret suns/They burn with passion, but only once."

"That's nice."

"I think he knew. I think he knew that never again would he feel anything like he felt for Rachel, so that's why he did it."

I bought one of their sickly sweet five-dollar coffees and sat in the window, watching the cars go by.

3:37 A.M.

I got out of bed and stomped down the stairs, wondering why that bitch was trying to provoke me by turning the TV up so goddamn loud.

When I got to the den the volume was absurd (Claude Rains, I noticed, *The Invisible Man*) but Rachel wasn't around. I cleared magazines off tables and felt under sofa cushions, but I couldn't find the remote anywhere.

"What are you doing?" Now she was in the doorway.

"I'm trying to turn this off."

"How did you turn it on?"

"I thought you did."

Rachel looked up at the wall-mounted TV. "Isn't there a power switch on there somewhere?"

"No. To put it on standby you need the remote." Finally I gave up and just yanked the cord out of the wall. I slid to the floor next to the socket, breathing heavily.

"How's the movie going?"

"Fine," I snapped.

"I was just asking."

She was in a t-shirt and panties. I could tell she hadn't waxed. Pornographic images of my wife and the face from the photographs flooded my mind. Bending, pounding, jiggling, moaning. I felt my anger rise. "What did you see in him?" I asked.

She sighed. "Not now, Alan."

But it was too late. I was getting a buzz of self-righteous indignation. "Did you do it in our bed? Did you try things with him that you don't with me? Did he read you his little poems afterward?"

"I said not now."

"He was a loser. Just another wannabe writer who'd never published a word. You can't throw a rock without hitting one of those in this town. None of them will ever amount to anything."

"Do you really want to know why I fucked a twenty-two-year-old poet?"

"Barista."

"Tabitha Kemp." The name hit me like a cold blast of air. "That's why. Tabitha Kemp. Even after eight years of marriage, you're still carrying a torch. And all this time I've had to live with the fact that I've never completely had you. Not completely." She stormed out of the room. I heard a door slam.

I closed my eyes and leaned my head against the wall. What could I say? She was right. Had Tabby ever left her husband and knocked on my door, I doubt my marriage to Rachel would have survived.

I got to my feet and went to the kitchen to put some coffee on. I found the remote in the refrigerator. I sure as hell didn't put it there.

I was following somebody through my house. Or maybe somebody was following me.

Footsteps. *Tap-tap-tap* on the Spanish tiles, always going up the stairs when I was in the hallway, or through the kitchen when I was in the den. Rooms were unusually cold. I felt I was being watched. Something was breathing.

I first heard the breathing in the dining room. I walked slowly around the heavy walnut table. The sound was always just on the other side. I stopped, it stopped. I sat down, watched the vacant space where I thought it was coming from, then kicked out one of the chairs. I don't know what the hell I was trying to accomplish by that.

Then the blackest and most catatonic despair I've ever felt dropped down on me like a veil. I shuffled into the kitchen and sat on the cold tiles with my back against the hard cabinets. I held my head in my hands. I moaned. Lupe, who was mopping over in the breakfast room, looked at me strangely.

"Meester Levy, *está bien?*"

I looked at her stupid, drooping face and crawled back to the dining room. I was losing my mind and I knew it. I lay down under the table and repeated my name over and over.

I don't remember falling asleep, but when I woke up I could feel Jeremy Rice in the house. I even knew where he was. He was in the downstairs guest room where Rachel had been sleeping. He was standing in the middle of the floor, waiting patiently for me.

I ran, not slowing down until I reached the door. By then my dream state was fading and I felt disoriented. My hand reached for the doorknob anyway. *I don't believe in ghosts*, I thought, then pushed the door open.

Blood. All over the walls. Coagulating gore, shit, bits of brain matter, part of a jaw. I stumbled backward out of the room, pulling the door shut with me. I think I was screaming, but it sounded like I was underwater. I was on the floor, then Lupe was there, calling "Meester Levy, Meester Levy!"

"Don't go in," I croaked.

"I just clean," she said. She reached for the doorknob despite my protestations. She pushed it open and looked inside. "*No es* nothing." She stepped out of the way and showed me. The room was spotless. When I looked back at her, I couldn't tell if her expression was one of pity or concern.

"I call Meessus Levy."

"No!" I said, struggling to my feet. "Don't call. I'm just going to go upstairs and lie down for a while."

Which I did, but the bedroom was spinning like I was drunk. It took all afternoon for it to finally stop.

From the notes of Dr. Yedida Kaufmann, PhD:

*Alan a no-show this week. Rachel said his film project has completely fallen apart. Had some kind of episode which she did not witness. Has become obsessed with home security, setting up cameras all over house, incl. hallway outside her room, and buying a 2 y.o. pit bull named Jaws. I said it's natural for jilted spouse to feel home has been invaded. Rachel seemed fidgety, uncertain.*

Night. I was in my study trying to distract myself with some dreadful rom com script Tony Brinker sent over when Jaws started to bark. Feeling my pulse race, I hurried into the den. He was snapping at the corner by the bookcase, like he'd trapped somebody there.

"Jaws, quiet!" I yelled, and he turned it down to a low growl. I grabbed a fireplace poker, I'm not sure why. I approached the dark corner, gripping it tightly. I heard breathing, and for a moment I was afraid of a repeat of last week. But this was different. I had the upper hand. I sensed him there, trapped and frightened, though I could see nothing. Barely above a whisper, I said, "Jeremy?"

Then Jaws whimpered and jumped backward, I heard footsteps running, and something fell and broke in the kitchen. I ran after him, Jaws at my heels. One of Rachel's decorative Mexican plates had fallen to the floor and shattered all over the tiles. I noticed a handprint on the sliding glass door. I went over to it. It was so small next to mine, almost feminine. As I watched, it started to disappear.

Suddenly I felt exhausted, drained. I leaned my forehead against the glass and let my breath fog it up. I looked out at the eerily-lit pool, and beyond that, the twinkling lights of Los Angeles. I once thought I would turn this city upside down. One star on the Walk of Fame wouldn't be enough for Alan Levy. Now I think I'd sell my soul to see my name on Hollywood Boulevard.

Funny, I thought. A Jew coveting a star.

The kitchen camera caught the whole thing. The plate was perfectly still, then it started to wobble, then it was in pieces so fast you almost didn't see it fall. The companion plate right above it never moved at all. There was no tremor last night. I believe I have captured conclusive video proof of supernatural infestation. This Jeremy Rice guy might just turn things around for me yet.

"We're getting nowhere," Rachel said. "We need to either fix this marriage, or end it."

I was in the middle of an email to Emma Watson, who had expressed interest in *We'll Always Have Wichita* (the dreadful rom com.) If she was on board, this thing would finance itself.

I quickly minimized the email. Rachel had just gotten back from Phoebe's house, and clearly their latest girl talk session had had more import than the Yalta Conference. (Or maybe the Wannsee Conference, I wasn't sure which yet.)

"This wasn't all my fault," she continued, sounding scripted. "In a successful marriage, both partners' needs must be met, and for a long time, mine were not being met."

I wasn't in the mood for this. "What is it you want me to do?" I asked.

She looked surprised by my compliance. She'd obviously expected a fight. "Well," she finally said, "You could start by coming to see Dr. Kaufmann again."

"Fine, I'll be there tomorrow." I waited for her to make more demands of me. Having none prepared, she left.

I brought up the email, and reading it over I realized why I'd guiltily minimized it when Rachel came in. I deleted the whole thing. I was coming across like a lecherous old man.

From the notes of Dr. Yedida Kaufmann, PhD:

*Very interesting session. Rachel said Alan is obsessed with idea that house is haunted by Jeremy Rice. Alan said plate fell from wall when no tremor, said Jeremy trying to communicate with him. Not her — him. I asked him what he thought Rice was trying to say. He looked at Rachel for a minute then said he didn't know.*

"I've sensed him too." I was in the kitchen making a sandwich. She approached me cautiously. "I don't think you're crazy."

"I wouldn't be so sure."

She took a few more steps in my direction. "Why is he here? Why is he trying to talk to you?"

I looked at her. God, she was beautiful. "Did you love him? I mean, really, really love him?"

"He made me feel like you did once," she said quietly. We were just inches apart now. I honestly don't remember who made the first move. Before I knew it we were back in our bed together for the first time in months. But the familiar wool of our intimacy was charged with a foreign static. As our bodies heated, the universe grew colder, and as our movements took on their own purpose she called out Jeremy's name. I didn't realize this until later, because in those accelerating minutes of self-immolation I *was* Jeremy Rice. His thoughts filled my head and my eyes saw only as he could see. I was saving Rachel, and Rachel was my salvation. Jeremy. I felt him moving through me, and in me, an anguished revenant flaying away at its own compulsion. I was pushed and pulled at once by hands much smaller than mine, stretched by skin much newer than mine, and just before the end came I saw our reflection in the framed *Jules and Jim* poster, and there were three of us on the bed, our arms and legs in a tangle, Jeremy and I moving in tandem like pistons, driven by the single-minded idea of *Rachel Rachel Rachel*. But I couldn't hold off any longer. I let it go, everything, all of it, then closed my eyes and dug my face into her neck. Rachel. Sleep beckoned, a black hole opened up behind my eyelids, and when I looked again she was smiling and stroking my face.

"Alan," she said. "Alan."

Jaws was barking. I was pulled out of Zulawski dreams to find my wife sleeping beside me. So normal, so strange. I ran downstairs, naked. The house was slanted all wrong. The light was sickly and pale. I smelled death. The alarm went off.

I found Jaws in the kitchen. The sliding glass door was open and Jaws was barking at the gap. I ran out onto the patio.

"What do you want?" I yelled.

The shimmering pool didn't answer me. Neither did the twinkling city lights nor the clear but starless sky. I shouted his name. Jeremy. I shouted Rachel's name; I shouted gibberish. I kept shouting until my voice failed me. I saw lights coming on across the terraced hillsides. Then Rachel was beside me, wearing a blanket. She wrapped me in it with her and led me back into the house, which was quiet and dark once more.

From the notes of Dr. Yedida Kaufmann, PhD:

*Incredible turnaround. Alan and Rachel report newfound commitment to marriage. Rachel says she wants to start writing again. Alan says he feels happier at home even if work still frustrates. Says Wichita fell through b/c Watson doing picture with "that fucking fincher" instead. (Note: what is a fincher?) I asked if one or both would write testimonials for website. Seemed open to idea.*

It's summer. The seasons change so gradually here a lot of people don't even notice. This isn't New England. The jasmine blooms pink, then white, and the rain beats its gradual northward retreat. The days get a little longer and warmer, but nothing too drastic. More people on the beach, more tops off the convertibles. The hills catch fire and slowly burn.

Our own rekindled flame flared quickly, then went out. I love my wife. I think she loves me back. We worked hard to save this marriage, but neither of us is defined by it, like some of our friends are defined by theirs. I try to imagine what Jeremy went through in his final days and hours, and I just can't. Did he toss and turn, unable to sleep, burning himself with cigarettes just to feel something besides the unbearable pain in his heart? Did I ever feel that way about Rachel? Rachel, who brings me mimosas when I sit by the pool at night, looking out over the city I once thought I'd conquer. Would I fling myself off that balcony if I couldn't have her? If I did, all those lights would just twinkle on indifferently. They've swallowed far greater giants than me.

I'm putting together a zombie picture and I've almost got Nick Cage, provided we can work around some scheduling issues. Every morning I take Santa Monica to my office, and every time I pass it my eyes find that Starbucks where Jeremy Rice filled notebooks with anguished words about my wife: his muse, his salvation, the reason he burned out in the full flame of youth, rather than let the comforting ice of age overtake him, bit by bit, like it does the rest of us. And in the afternoon I pass it again.

Back and forth, every day. Passion, indifference, push and pull. I can still flare, but not for long. Every star you see is already gone.

Addison Clift's *fiction has appeared in places such as* Shock Totem, Grim Corps, Not One of Us, *and* The Future Fire. *He lives (and tries to find time to write) in Vermont.*

# THE GROTESQUE

## Rhonda Parrish

The breath of the house rushes
from your bedroom window
and pours over my hide like water.
It warms my twisted form,
melting the early morning frost from my spine.
A caress, lending me strength,
hope,
because the house knows.

It knows what the dark conceals,
it watches every night,
watches and shivers
and fears.
It groans in sympathy.
The sound fills it, fr-om cellar to attic
but you don't hear.
Sleeping, comfortable and content
on the safe side of the glass,
you never hear.

Come dawn you open your window,
examine me, perched on your sill.
You marvel at the deep crack on my wing,
the jagged piece absent from my claw.
You wonder, think it a great mystery,
but the house knows.

The house knows.

Rhonda Parrish *is driven by a desire to do All The Things. She has been the publisher and editor-in-chief of* Niteblade Magazine *for over five years now (which is like 25 years in internet time) and is the editor of the forthcoming* World Weaver Press *anthology,* Fae.

*In addition, Rhonda is a writer whose work has been included or is forthcoming in dozens of publications including* Tesseracts 17: Speculating Canada from Coast to Coast, Mythic Delirium, *and of course,* Bete Noire.

*Her website, updated weekly, is at* http://www.rhondaparrish.com.

TRACES IN LIGHT *by Mark A. France*

*With a penchant for graveyard photography and necro-tourism trips around his home state of Michigan,* **Mark A. France** *still sleeps with his baby blanket and avoids looking out the back window of his bedroom late at night, for fear that he may see something moving amongst the shadows. Yet, these fears play heavily into his writing, which often focus on macabre tales woven with the patchwork of the human condition. From ghosts to corpses raised from the grave,* **France** *takes simple situations and laces them with complex characters in terrifying settings, brought to life by his unique style of writing. France is also an avid photographer and award-winning filmmaker.*

# GENE PUDDLE

## Matthew Fryer

"Morning." Bader flashed his ID to the young clerk on the door.

"Good afternoon."

"Oh, is it?"

She raised a slightly admonishing eyebrow. "The graduation ceremony finished over an hour ago."

"I got stuck in traffic. Anybody left?"

"Just a handful of ticking time-bombs, I'm afraid."

"So it's a weak heart or a pervert?"

"Pretty much. What's your industry?"

"Meat-packing. I need a new line manager. The last one died in a house fire."

"I'm sorry to hear that."

"His DNA was squeaky clean, too. Could've worked until he was seventy-five."

"What a waste. Well, let's see what we've got. I take it you don't need an academic."

"Nah. Just somebody with a bit of common sense who can sort out the rotas and keep the factory floor boneheads from burning the place down."

"That should be doable. This way."

The clerk led him through an arched doorway into the university de-gowning chamber and Bader wilted at the leftover youths, clutching vending machine coffees and grumbling amongst themselves like stranded tourists at an airport. "Is this it?"

"'Fraid so. It's been a busy afternoon and we're about to pack the stragglers off to labour distribution."

"Okay." Bader's eye was drawn to a pretty girl flirting with one of the other clerks, all sheets of black hair and deep, doe eyes. "What about her?"

"Akemi Hayashi. She graduated in business management and ticks all the boxes, other than she's got a brain full of aneurysms like balloon animals. She could pop in the next five seconds. If she's lucky, she might see a year."

"Doesn't she qualify for terminal inform?"

"If she knew, the stress would kill her in a week. Her blood pressure's controlled, and that's all anybody can do. Although she's starting to wonder why she's still here."

"I'll pass. I can't be bothered with the fallout when she finally susses it out."

"Fair enough." The clerk nodded to a grey-suited girl with a severe fringe snapping into her phone. "Nina Payne's probably your best shot. Got a solid degree and her parents work in haulage, so she's more than used to *factory floor boneheads* as you call them."

"What's the catch?"

"The word on the chromosomes is a good chance of psychosis and a red flag for t-cell leukaemia."

"Shelf life?"

"About four years."

"Okay, she's a maybe." Bader turned towards a well-built unshaven boy lolling in the corner who looked as though he'd found his suit in a skip. "He looks like foreman material."

"Doug Stackhouse. Strong and bright but a genetic predisposition to alcoholism and depression."

Doug's wet eyes betrayed a mother of a hangover and Bader bet he'd downed a couple of schooners for breakfast to take the edge off it. "Any other problems?"

"He hasn't actually *done* anything illegal yet but his holistic profile red-flagged him for police observation. Apparently there's a good chance of sexual deviance, probably paedophilia."

"I'll take him."

"Really?"

"Strong and bright, you said, and the boneheads won't mess with a big stocky boozer like him."

"True, but when the drinking and depression hit a trough you'll be lucky if he does much work."

"So he gets shitfaced and falls in the industrial grinder. Or *throws* himself in. Either way, we get a free carcass and I can sue his estate for damages. And best of all, I don't have to lose any sleep over a dead child molester."

"Fair enough. I'll go and sort the paperwork." The clerk glanced across at Doug and smiled. "And judging by the state of him, I imagine we'll be seeing you again pretty soon."

"Probably." Bader sighed. "I'll try and be early next time."

Matthew Fryer *lives with his wife in Sheffield, England, and works in the windowless basement of his local hospital. As well as reading and writing fiction, he likes ska music, chillies and Rollercoaster Tycoon 3. Visit his website - The Hellforge - at* www.matthewfryer.com

# His Unsecured Love

## WC Roberts

Taylor stoops over his project, adjusting his top hat
he taps a speck of dust from his checkered jacket
and replaces the wilted 'mum in his lapel

She'd been his love, his everything
and couldn't take what age was doing to her
she begged him to help her

he snaps on the r-light and watches them
ripple beneath the skin, a herd of pupae grazing
yellow subcutaneous fat
and her beauty slips off like a glove
that he puts on.  "My love," with fingertips
brushing wisps of errant hair back under his hat
"we'll be together always," he says
"and you'll never change
nor will I
change you."  Her skin, in tatters, clings to him still
and all that he said, all that he was
trails behind them now--
a cloud of flies buzzing jovial
hurling bolts of lightning into the pincushions
of adversity, the ticking of a clock
its face tattooed with numbers
*ad nauseam,* incomplete.

WC Roberts *lives in a mobile home up on Bixby Hill, on land that was once the county dump. The only window looks out on a ragged scarecrow standing in a field of straw and dressed in WC's own discarded clothes. WC dreams of the desert, of finally getting his first television set, and of ravens. Above all, he writes, and has had poems published in* **Strange Horizons, Apex, Space & Time Magazine, Mindflights, Aoife's Kiss, Big Pulp, Star\*Line,** *and others.*

CAROSEL *by Luke Spooner*

Luke Spooner *a.k.a. 'Carrion House' currently lives and works in the South of England. Having recently graduated from the University of Portsmouth with a first class degree he is now a full time illustrator for just about any project that peaks his interest. Despite regular forays into children's books and fairy tales his true love lies in anything macabre, melancholy or dark in nature and essence. He believes that the job of putting someone else's words into a visual form, to accompany and support their text, is a massive respons-ibility as well as being something he truly treasures.*

*www.carrionhouse.com*
*www.facebook.com/carrionhouse*

# Walking With Sina

## Marge Simon

My windows are laced with scarlet ice. Below in the barren street, the statue leers, blind witness to the slaughter ten nights ago. Sina is restless. She begs to take an evening walk. Her hair is smoke, silver slivers dance in her eyes. She weaves a strand of nonsense chatter as I follow her, hands tucked deep into the pockets of my cloak. I have brought the gun, for it may as well be now. Our boots crunch along a thin layer of sidewalk ice.

"Don't be so bitter," she says. "You've lost your gods. I'll make you new ones."

*Sina, my own, what have you become? The soldiers, the blood. You liked it all, despite the noise. Even what they did to the children.*

She darts ahead on tiptoe, the scuttle of dead leaves and spider trails, where only shadows grow. I know the signs. The night sky overflows with mystic orbs. We near the totem. Phantoms play across its sable veneer. Ancestral images displaced by scalding lights. Wendigo or Manitou, which is it, my Sina?

We pause beneath, our breaths form pink crystals atomized by torch lights. "There is no totem here," she laughs, and with a sweet blue-white flash of thigh, she leaps to ride the dragon. Silhouetted in gossamer lights, she stands, waving to the stars.

*I have one bullet left in the pistol. Sina is the last of her kind. But I love her to death.*

Marge Simon's *works appear in publications such as* Strange Horizons, Niteblade, DailySF Magazine, Pedestal Magazine, Dreams & Night-mares. *She edits a column for the HWA Newsletter and serves as Chair of the Board of Trustees. She has won the Strange Horizons Readers Choice Award, the Bram Stoker Award™(2008, 2012, 2013), the Rhysling Award and the Dwarf Stars Award. Collections:* Like Birds in the Rain, Unearthly Delights, The Mad Hattery, Vampires, Zombies & Wanton Souls, *and* Dangerous Dreams. Member HWA, SFWA, SFPA. *www.margesimon.com*

Subscribe to

# BÊTE NOIRE

## 1 year, 4 issues
## $23.95*

Send email to: subscribe @betenoiremagazine.com

Or fill out the form below and send, along with check or
money order made payable to Jennifer Gifford to:

P.O. Box 1545
Highland, MI 48357

Name:_____

Address: _____

Email:_____

Susbcription includes Dark Opus Press's annual anthology

*US and Canada only, international subscriptions $29.95/year